Tekoa Justice

The Best Thing About Christmas!

Written By
Christine Harder Tangvald

Illustrated by
Judy Hand

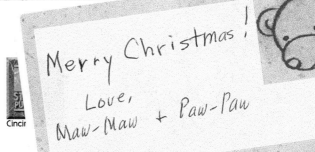

Merry Christmas!
Love,
Maw-Maw + Paw-Paw

Cincir

First hardcove
Text © 1990 by Chris
Illustrations © 1990 by The S͟... ͟.͟.͟.͟.͟.͟.͟.͟.͟ishing Company
The Standard Publishing Company, Cincinnati, Ohio. A division of Standex International Corporation

Designed by Coleen Davis
ISBN 0-7847-0850-9. Library of Congress Catalog Card Number 89-52035

I like everything about Christmas, don't you?

I like to decorate our Christmas tree with silver tinsel, and pretty ornaments, and tiny lights that wink and blink, blink and wink.

And I like to put shiny round balls on our Christmas tree—red ones, and blue ones, and green ones, and yellow ones. Decorating our Christmas tree is fun!

But that's not the BEST thing about Christmas.

I like all the colors of Christmas!

Blue and green packages tied with bows made of satin ribbon, and snowy white candles to light with a match, and bright yellow stars that twinkle and shine through the night, and striped red candy canes stuffed in our Christmas stockings.

Oh, yes. I like the colors of Christmas.

But that's not the BEST thing about Christmas.

I like all the special words we use at **Christmas.**

Ho Ho Ho!
and
"JOY to the world!"

and
**"MERRY
CHRISTMAS,
everyone!"**

And I like all the things we do at
Christmas to help other people.
We care and share.

We shake hands and smile
and say, "Hello! How ARE you?
It's so good to see you."

It makes me feel good when I care
and share with other people.

But that's not the BEST thing about Christmas.

I like all the good foods we eat at **Christmas**.

Pretty sugar cookies with red and green frosting and sprinkles on the top.

Yum, YUM!

And turkey with dressing and cranberry sauce and pumpkin pie with lots of whipped cream for dessert.

Yum, yum, YUM!

And big round oranges,
and chocolate fudge,
and gooey, chewy gumdrops!

Yum, yum, YUM!

I love gooey,
chewy gumdrops!

**But that's not
the BEST thing
about Christmas.**

I like the sounds of Christmas.

Christmas bells ringing,
DING, DONG, DING!

People singing—

FA, la la la LA, la LA, LA, LA!

And I like the smells of Christmas.

The fresh smell of our pine wreath hanging on the front door, and the smell of Mom's apple pie baking in the oven.

**Mmmm.
Mmmm. Good.**

But that's still not the BEST thing about Christmas.

And I like the time we spend together at Christmas.

Eating together, shopping together, reading together, praying together, and just talking together.

Being together at Christmas is nice. But that's not the BEST thing about Christmas, either!

Then what IS the best thing about Christmas?

I think the BEST thing about Christmas is . . .

JESUS!
BABY JESUS!

Yes, Jesus is the best thing about Christmas.

You see, Christmas is Jesus' birthday, and did you know that Jesus is God's own Son? He is.

Jesus is God's very own Son!

Long ago, baby Jesus was born
in a stable in a little town
called Bethlehem.
Mary was Jesus' mother.
Joseph was there, too.

He took good care of Mary
and baby Jesus.

It was God's plan.

That first Christmas night,
God sent beautiful angels to tell the shepherds
about his Son, Jesus.

"Glory to God in the highest!"

sang the angels!

The shepherds
were surprised,
and ...

. . . they left their flocks of sheep out in the fields and came to Bethlehem to worship Jesus.

The shepherds loved baby Jesus.

And did you know that Jesus came into this world for me, too? He did. He really, really did. Isn't that wonderful? Jesus came for me.

Thank you, God, for Christmas.
Happy birthday, Jesus!

Yes, I like everything about Christmas.
But I think the BEST thing is . . .

Jesus
came
for
me!